MW00937241

They Call Me Mommy

The Tail Tale Of
An Eastern Gray Squirrel

written by
Bonnie Lee Strunk

illustrated by
James E. Brasted

authorHOUSE™

1663 LIBERTY DRIVE, SUITE 200
BLOOMINGTON, INDIANA 47403
(800) 839-8640
WWW.AUTHORHOUSE.COM

First published by AuthorHouse 10/27/05

ISBN: 1-4208-8512-X (sc)

Printed in the United States of America
Bloomington, Indiana

This book is printed on recycled, acid-free paper.

for Mommy,
who inspires and teaches

for Jimbo,
who shares my love
of the natural world

Chapter One

Delta ran into the house, yelling for her dad. "Come! Quick! Look at the squirrel. It has its mouth full of leaves!" she called.

Three curious faces appeared at the back window, staring out at me. Through the glass I could hear their excited voices.

"What's it doing with the leaves?" asked Darby, Delta's younger brother.

"Probably building a nest," replied their father. "I'll bet it's a female, and she's looking for a place to raise a family."

Delta and Darby jumped up and down with glee, as I have seen human children do many times.

Their father was right. I had been feeling desperate to find a home -- a cozy, safe nest where I could raise my first litter of babies. But I couldn't find a tree.

That old maple with a high-up hollow where a dead limb was cut off years ago had been a wonderful home. In fact, it was where my brothers and I were born, just last year.

But the tree is gone now, along with all the rest of that stand of sturdy oaks and majestic maples and the huge beech that provided us with delicious nuts in the fall.

Our snug homes, as well as our food supply, had to make way for more "people" houses, so now we're all scrambling to find new places to live.

With more and more land stripped to build houses and roads and shopping centers, we wild animals are having a rough time finding food and shelter and places to raise our young. As our natural habitat dwindles, homes for us become scarce, and competition for them becomes keen.

During play one day I happened to spy a bird checking out a hole in a dilapidated porch ceiling, right next door to the house where Delta and Darby live. Curious, I took a peek after the bird flew off. Not bad. That space had possibilities for a squirrel, I thought.

Now something stirred deep within me, urging

me to build a nest at once. I know I must follow my instincts.

I gathered as many leaves as I could stuff into my mouth at one time and headed for that hole in the second floor porch ceiling. Getting up there was not easy.

First I had to climb the shingles on the back of the building. Thankfully my sharp claws can cling to the siding. Then I had to make my way over the rain gutter and onto the porch floor.

Now I was ready to climb the thick pole that supported the third floor porch above me. Around the top of the pole, where the wood had rotted away, was an opening just big enough for me to crawl into. This would make a safe, dry home for my little ones and me.

I left the leaves in my new home and headed back out for more nesting material. For over an hour I worked, until my little chest heaved with weariness. Up I climbed, with a mouthful of leaves and a piece of paper bag and a small strip of red cloth, then down again I came to search for more bedding that would keep my nest soft and warm.

CHAPTER TWO

A s Delta and Darby watched, they knew their dad had been right. "She's going in that hole next door, where the blackbird lived last year," Delta reported. "Do you think the squirrel will have babies there, like the bird did?" Just the thought of it caused her to jump up and down again with excitement.

They were nice kids. They enjoyed watching me and made sure I had nuts and seeds and water. Healthy food was necessary so that I could nourish my infants. Right now, pizza crusts and stale bread that neighbors sometimes threw out for the birds (which I ate, too, when I was hungry) would not be good enough.

Darby was bursting with curiosity. "Think she

had her babies yet, Dad? When will we get to see them?" He asked this question every day.

His father, a gentle, bearded man, was patient. "She looks a bit bigger to me, Darby, so my guess is she probably has a few little ones up there that she's nursing. We have to make sure she has fresh water to drink, because she has to produce milk for the babies."

Delta, about ten years old, was a bright girl who loved to learn something new. She checked the library for books about gray squirrels, and read that my babies would be born tiny, about the size of a human thumb, and blind and hairless. Their fur would begin to grow when the babies were one to two weeks old, but they would not open their eyes and ear flaps until they were about five weeks old.

"Dad, the book says she probably would have from one to five babies. How many do you think are up there?"

"No idea, dear," he replied. "We'll just have to wait until they start moving around. And that won't happen until they're about six or seven weeks old. That's what your book says."

Delta and Darby carefully watched the hole in the porch ceiling. It was the first place they looked when they got out of bed every morning. When they were outdoors, they looked up often, hoping to catch a glimpse of me or my little ones.

Fortunately these human neighbors, who call me "Mommy," enjoy squirrels. Some people, I have heard, do not like squirrels. They call us rodents. But that's not a bad word. Indeed, that is what we are.

We are members of the rodentia order, which includes a great many mammal species. Fellow rodents, close relatives of ours, include chipmunks, hamsters, prairie dogs, beavers, groundhogs and mice.

The word rodent comes from the Latin word "rodere," which means "to gnaw." How appropriate. All rodents do gnaw, not to be nasty or destructive, but because that is how we were made. Gnawing on hard objects is biologically necessary. It keeps our continually-growing teeth sharp and short and useable.

CHAPTER THREE

As my little ones grew, they were getting restless in their cramped nest. At six weeks old, they were ready for a peek at the outside world.

Cautiously, the largest and boldest of the litter poked her nose out of the hole. Wide-eyed, she was fascinated by all she saw and turned her tiny head back and forth to watch flying birds and hovering bumblebees. But she was easily frightened, so whenever she saw a human or heard a dog bark or a horn blow, she darted back inside to the safety of her nest and siblings.

Her brother and two sisters were not as eager to follow her lead. They liked the security of their home, hidden from the world outside. But like human youngsters, they were overcome with curiosity, and they, too, finally took a look.

Then one day it happened. Delta was gazing up at the hole just at the moment my little ones were moving around in their nest.

"A tail!" she shouted. "Darby, I just saw a skinny tail. It must be a baby!"

From then on, the children and their father watched for a glimpse of my babies. Their persistence was rewarded.

As long as the humans were indoors, peering through the glass, my babies played freely, darting in and out of the hole, climbing the pole a few inches, testing their claws and their balance.

Delta never tired of watching my amusing youngsters and their antics. After a week of observation, she was pretty sure I had had four babies. She was right.

"I think we should give them names," she told her family. "They all look a little different."

To Delta and Darby, my oldest and bravest became known as Pumpkin. Funny, she didn't look anything like a big orange pumpkin to me! They named the others Peanut, Pixie and Pippin. Pippin was my only boy.

Although once in a while I heard the human children referring to one of my offspring by the wrong name, most of the time Delta and Darby were quite good at telling the little ones apart.

Being new in my mommy role, it was hard for me to keep a watchful eye on all four of my active, inquisitive infants, especially when they were climbing up and down the pole and exploring the second floor porch.

Naturally I could not be with the babies every minute. After all, I had to eat and drink lots of water so that I could feed them. Sometimes I just needed a break, so I rested on the wooden bench in the children's yard next door. And I had to keep a watch out for that red-tailed hawk that often lurked in the neighborhood. How he would love to eat baby squirrels for lunch!

CHAPTER FOUR

One afternoon when I returned to my nest, Pixie was missing. I popped back out immediately and looked across the porch. She wasn't there. I scurried down to the concrete patio and searched behind the trash can and the air conditioner unit. I looked in a nearby shrub. No Pixie.

Frantic, I sat on the wooden fence and called out, alternating my message between alarm and scolding. Where was she? What had happened?

Up and down I ran, checking along one side of the fence, then the other. Why didn't Pixie come when she heard my call?

The children next door heard me and came running outside to investigate. "What's wrong, Mommy? Why are you so upset?" pleaded Delta, holding out a walnut. I ignored the nut and continued my cries.

"Listen," instructed Darby. "I think I hear something." They stood still and listened. So did I. Soon all of us heard a faint scratching sound coming from somewhere nearby. Could it be my Pixie?

Delta hurried into the house and came out with her father. "Listen, Dad. I think something might be stuck in the rain spout next door. We heard a scratching noise." He listened, and soon he heard it, too.

Since the first floor apartment tenants were away on vacation, the children's dad took control. Quickly he walked next door, with Delta and Darby following closely behind. From atop the fence, I could not take my eyes off them.

"I'll disconnect the bottom section and see if something is trapped," he said, pulling the metal apart easily. "The opening at the end is so bent, nothing could escape that way. I'm surprised even water can get through."

When he had separated the spouting, he placed it on the ground. I held my breath. Nothing happened.

Finally he shook it a little as he turned it upside down, and out fell my Pixie, black as coal.

Terrified, she ran down the yard, with me in close pursuit. How horrible it would have been if she had remained trapped in there. I shudder to think about it.

Delta and Darby were ecstatic. "You saved the baby, Dad," they shouted.

"I don't know which one it was. It ran away so fast and was all dirty," Darby said. "I hope Mommy finds her baby."

He need not have worried. I found Pixie huddled beneath the holly bush, shaking with fear. Together we snuggled until she was calm and I could try to get her back to the nest.

Meanwhile, the children's dad was on a ladder, putting a little wire basket that he called a gutter guard over the hole where the rain gutter meets the downspout. "Now no birds or animals can get in there again. The baby squirrel must have fallen from its nest or from the porch and went right down the spouting. That would have been a terrible way to die," he told his son and daughter. "That's why we have these guards in all our downspouts. They're like the safety caps on our chimneys. They keep animals safe."

Pixie followed me, but she could not climb the siding on the back of the building. Each time she tried to get up to our home, she fell down. Darkness was approaching and the other babies were hungry. Finally I picked her up by her belly and carried her in my mouth as I struggled to reach our nest.

Even though she weighed only a few ounces, I myself weighed just over one pound, so Pixie was a heavy load. I managed to climb the wooden fence and the siding on the apartment building, but then I had to rest on the second floor porch.

While I lay there, trying to get more strength, Pixie scampered around the porch floor and, spotting a new plastic tablecloth on the small metal table in the corner, grabbed the end of it in her teeth and tugged. My other three youngsters peered down from their nest with interest and a bit of impatience. We'll be up soon, I assured them. And we were.

CHAPTER FIVE

If Pippin were a human boy, I am positive he would be a musician. On the porch below our nest hang wind chimes that have fascinated him ever since he began exploring the world outside his home.

Whenever I hear the soft melody of chimes, I have to check whether it is a windy day or whether Pippin is performing one of his concerts.

His musical talent did not escape the children's notice. Watching from the back window, Delta was amazed to see him hanging by his back feet as he joyfully batted the metal pipes with his front paws.

"Maybe Pippin is trying to play the 'Nutcracker Suite'," she joked to her brother.

CHAPTER SIX

My babies were seeking more and more adventure. Peanut, the tiniest of the four, tested her bravery one afternoon by climbing all the way down the pole to the porch floor. I let her go; as long as she ventured no farther, she was safe.

Getting back up to our home was another matter, however. Whenever she climbed a few inches, she slid down to the bottom. This went on for hours.

I could see that she had not yet learned how to fully use her sharp claws. In addition, she did not have the strength to pull herself up.

As the day wore on, I was expecting to have to go down and carry her back. But she was a determined little gal.

"I think I can. I think I can," she whispered. And finally, as nightfall approached, she did.

CHAPTER SEVEN

Pumpkin was the first to willingly climb all the way down to the ground for real exploration. After watching me from the safety of our home for a few weeks, she knew I drank from a large water dish (actually the top part of a bird bath that set on Delta's patio) and ate nuts and seeds from a feeder that had a lid I could open by pushing up with my head.

Delta and Darby's father had installed the feeder to keep the birds from taking all my nuts. Often when the children threw peanuts on the ground, the bluejays and crows would swoop down and fly off with my meal before I could get very much.

Of course, he had bird feeders, too, and ears of dried corn hanging from small chains in the backyard tree. There was plenty to eat for all of us critters. The small serviceberry tree had delicious berries, too, and the old black walnut tree in a neighboring yard provided a bounty of nuts to bury for winter. The white oak tree in Delta's yard was too young to produce acorns, but someday it would.

After hours of watching me, Pumpkin thought she knew how to drink from the big dish. I wasn't so sure. I still remember the first time I tried to drink water. I almost drowned!

Sure enough, Pumpkin put her entire face into the water and came up sneezing and coughing. Only one such experience is necessary to teach a lesson. Unafraid, she wiped her face with her front paws and tried again. This time only her little pink tongue dipped into the surface of the water.

Proud of her new success, she darted through the yard, leaping like a bunny. How cool and soft the grass felt on her paws. I know.

I remember my first time on the ground and how I ran and jumped with happiness. But I can't forget the danger that awaited me that day, too.

In another yard I had found a discarded black plastic tray that had diamond-shaped holes in it. I later heard the children's dad say it was a tray used to carry plants home from the garden shop.

Anyway, the new "toy" I had found and was playing with almost killed me. I somehow got stuck in one of the holes – I was much smaller at eight weeks old than I am now – and in my panic I tried to escape through the chain link fence at the back of the yard. Now I was stuck in the tray and the tray was stuck in the fence.

Fortunately Darby heard my loud cries and investigated. Even more fortunately, his dad came with a pair of clippers and snipped the plastic tray to free me. I am forever grateful to that wonderful man. Stuck there, I would have been easy prey for hungry hawks or cats or other animals. I often wonder whether the family realizes that I, Mommy, am the same squirrel they saved when I was just a baby.

Like her mom, Pumpkin got into trouble her first time on the ground. In her zeal to test her climbing ability, or maybe to show off, she jumped onto the wooden trellis on which red-flowered honeysuckle grows. Somehow she got her left back foot caught between two slats of wood and could not get loose. I heard her frightened whimpers and came running, but I had no idea how to help her. So I added my cries to hers, and soon Delta came out to see what the fuss was about.

She ran back to the house to get her father. "I'll have to take out the screw holding these boards together," he told the children, as he tried unsuccessfully to pry the wood apart enough to let her escape. As soon as the screw was loosened, Pumpkin was free again and scurried off without a limp.

I stuck around to try to show the humans my gratitude. I hope they understood.

CHAPTER EIGHT

Delta was startled but delighted to look out her kitchen window one morning and see Peanut sitting on the sill, looking in at her. The day was stormy, and Peanut had her bushy tail spread over her head like an umbrella, protecting her from the rain.

From her reading and observations, Delta knew that we squirrels use our fluffy tails in a variety of ways. Our tails give us balance and help us steer during tightrope acts on overhead wires and pencil-thin branches.

Besides shielding us from wet weather, our tails become blankets to cover our backs when the days turn cold.

CHAPTER NINE

"Delta, there must be a hawk around here somewhere. Listen to Mommy!" Darby called to his sister.

He was wrong, and Delta soon told him so. "No, that's not the sound Mommy makes when she sees a hawk. She must be seeing a cat. And look, she's twirling her tail, too."

Delta's attention to detail was evident. She could distinguish among my various cries and knew what each one meant. She was right. I did see a large yellow cat, another stray that roams the city streets, and I was warning my youngsters and other animals of the danger. It's too bad cats are not kept indoors where they belong. House cats are not part of the natural environment.

Cats are predators and can tear squirrels and songbirds and other wildlife to pieces. My loud

"CRRK....CRRK....CRRK....RAAA," which Darby said resembles a duck quacking, was the scolding, chattering sound I make when a cat is nearby.

"When Mommy sees a hawk, Darby, she makes a very soft cry, almost like a little kitten's meow," Delta proudly explained, sharing her knowledge with her little brother. "And she stays real still, almost frozen in place. She doesn't twitch her tail."

I was proud of Delta. She has become my interpreter.

CHAPTER TEN

"**C**an we make a Mother's Day card, Daddy?" Delta asked. Her father stared at her. The children's mother had died, I knew, so why was Delta asking such a question?

"It's for Mommy," Delta continued. "She's a mother, you know, so we should give her a card on her special day."

Their father laughed. "Sure, but don't be surprised if she ignores it. She's not that interested in anything she can't eat," he explained.

From the wooden fence I watched the children create their colorful art. With folded paper and crayons, they worked at the picnic table in the backyard.

On the front of the card was a drawing of a big squirrel (guess who?), surrounded by four fat, fuzzy little ones.

One youngster they colored mostly brown, with white paws. That would be my Peanut. Even though we are called gray squirrels, we are not always gray. Some of us are tan or brown or black or a combination of colors. I've even seen a silly squirrel with a gray body and a cinnamon-colored tail.

Darby colored another one light gray, with huge black eyes. That must be Pixie. The other two were colored both brown and gray, with some white hairs in their tails, so I could not tell which was supposed to be Pippin and which was Pumpkin, since both of them are multi-colored.

Inside was a sweet greeting which Darby recited while Delta wrote: "Happy Mother's Day, Mommy! We love you and your babies." It was signed by both the children.

Before trying to give the card to me, they showed it to their dad. "Nice artwork," he said. "Good job. I think she'll like it."

Delta put the card on the lawn and waited. Curious to find out what it smelled like, I ran over and sniffed. I looked at it and sniffed it again. Definitely it was not edible! I looked up into their faces. I hope they could tell I appreciated their thoughtfulness. Gazing into their eyes was my way of thanking them.

Darby put a large walnut on the ground, and I eagerly picked it up and twirled it in my front paws. I do this to make sure there is a nut inside the shell and to feel how heavy it is. This was a good one!

CHAPTER ELEVEN

"I just noticed something," Darby said to Delta. "Mommy has four fingers on her front paws and five on the back. Think something is wrong with her?"

I knew the answer, of course, but I let Delta respond. She went into the house for her book.

"It says here, Darby, that squirrels have four flexible toes on their front feet and five on their rear feet. They also have sweat glands on the bottom of their feet, so they don't get overheated in the summer," Delta recited.

"You're becoming real experts on squirrels," the children's father declared. "You're teaching me a lot. Isn't this a fun way to learn about nature?"

"I'm learning so much by watching them, Dad," Delta replied. "I love when the babies play together. They jump on each other and wrestle and run around and around the tree trunks playing hide and seek. They act just like little kids. Sometimes one little squirrel jumps on the seat of the swing and goes for a ride. That's funny."

Delta remembered another comical sight and started laughing. "Yesterday I saw one little guy – I couldn't tell which one – batting the flowers. Those big round allium balls must have looked like a toy, and the baby squirrel was leaping up in the air and boxing with the flower heads. Watching the squirrels is more fun than watching TV!"

Darby added, "My favorite thing is when Mommy yawns and stretches, just like people do. She is so silly when she hangs by her back feet and stretches out one front paw and then the other."

"Watching Mommy, I've learned what a great, protective mother she is," Delta observed. "And it's fun to see the babies grow and learn new things, just like human babies. But squirrel infants grow up much faster."

CHAPTER TWELVE

"Why are squirrels here, Dad? What's their purpose?" Darby asked.

"That's a good question, son. What do you think?" asked his father.

It was a good question, one which all of us – animals and humans alike – could ask.

Perhaps we squirrels were created to plant trees, to make sure that no matter how many trees are lost to development or logging, the world will never be without this important part of nature.

Many of the nuts and pine cones we bury are forgotten, and eventually they sprout as saplings, planted by us.

Maybe we are here to aerate the soil. Our sharp claws make great little shovels when we're burying or digging up tasty treasures. Humans who watch us are fascinated by the way we use our teeth, front paws and noses to bury our goodies and then very carefully pat down the soil and leaves or sticks to cover our hidden food supply.

Some people, such as my wonderful neighbors Delta, Darby and their dad, really don't care why squirrels are here. They're just glad we are and willingly share this land with us and with all fellow creatures.

Observing us, the most visible of wild critters, can teach the human family much about the natural world and animal behavior.

We can help people discover the connection between humans and animals, and how the choices people make can positively or negatively impact the lives of not only squirrels, but all wildlife.

When human youngsters get to know their native wildlife, as Delta and Darby are doing, they will be better able to understand the responsibility everyone has to take care of our earth. That will benefit all of us who live here – animals and people.

But enough of MY answer. Darby finally came up with his own.

"I think squirrels are here, Dad, because they're clever and cute and intelligent and entertaining," he announced.

I won't argue with that.

THE END

ABOUT THE AUTHOR

Since childhood, Bonnie Lee Strunk has been captivated by the beauty and magic of nature. Raised in a rural area of Pennsylvania, she became an avid observer of wildlife and especially loves squirrels, which she considers to be the most fascinating and friendly critters in the wild animal kingdom.

The author holds a B.A. degree in journalism from Temple University and an M.A. degree from Kutztown University. She teaches writing workshops and grammar refresher classes, and for more than 30 years has been writing for newspapers and magazines. She has won numerous state and national journalism and photography awards.

A regular columnist for a chain of weekly newspapers in Pennsylvania, she often writes articles focused on nature and the importance of being good stewards of the earth.

She and her husband, a retired professor and "weekend" artist who provided the drawings for this book, are trained Habitat Ambassadors for the National Wildlife Federation. As volunteers, they visit garden centers, church groups, retirement communities and other forums, presenting programs on the benefits of native plants and gardening for wildlife. They also teach ecology workshops for children and donate native trees to public spaces.

In addition, Bonnie Lee Strunk has written and performs "Animal Rap," a rap song with a message to all of us from our animal friends.

Her favorite pastimes include nature photography, cooking and playing the baroque recorder.

Printed in the United States
46785LVS00002B/1-60

9 781420 885125